THE *Boyfriend* BARGAIN

By

Tizahmi

Copyright

This is a work of fiction. Names, characters, businesses, places, events, and incidents are either the products of the author's imagination or used in a fictitious manner. Any resemblance to actual persons, living or dead, or actual events is purely coincidental.

Acknowledgments

This book was another labor of love. I write this for all who have found love and happiness in the least likely of places and circumstances.

To my family, know that your continued support helped me to stay focused and meet my deadlines. A special thank you to Jerry, who helped calm the turbulent waves of my mind, making it possible for me to accomplish so much, a proven friend, my muse.

For all my other friends and colleagues who have shared in my excitement to see this book completed, thank you for pushing me.

Chapter One

The conference room was eerily quiet. Lauren had purposely let them all sit there, racking their brains to figure out what was going on. With as controlled a voice as her anger would allow, smoking eyes momentarily rested on each of them, "It was brought to my attention that this group didn't bother to double-check the financial reports handed over to the CEO regarding the Trident Inc. account."

Bodies now started to shift in several of the chairs around the conference table. "Due to your carelessness, this firm may have just lost the opportunity to secure one of this State's leading publicly traded companies. Also, I now have to personally figure out just how to persuade them to reconsider working with us here at Myers Financial Services."

"Uhm, what can we do to help? I mean, since we messed up, we should be the ones to fix this," said a half-quiet voice. It was Janet, one of the interns, whom Lauren knew the others stuck with most of the grunt work. Still, she never failed to have a warm smile on her face and didn't complain.

I need to see about getting this one on permanent. As for the others, this crisis will determine just who will be out on their ass by the end of this month. The 25th was the day Trident Inc. representatives were coming back for a final meeting. *Two weeks is all the time these "geniuses" have; sink or swim!*

"Well, Janet, you're correct. All of you, and not just Janet, will start from scratch and have your completed reports on my desk within the next 14 days. That will leave me with five to review and work on the rest of the presentation. Oh, and yes, 14 days, counting the weekends. I hope you don't have anything planned, as you all will be practically living in this building."

Lauren waved her right hand at the group, signaling they were dismissed. She waited until the last possible moment before calling out to Janet,

"Janet, please stay. I'd like to go over some things

with you.”

“Oh yes, sure.”

Once the conference room door closed, Lauren looked up from the journal she’d been making notes in. Janet just sat straight-backed in her chair, hands in her lap.

“Do relax, dear. You are not personally in any trouble. I wanted to say that I noticed all the work you’ve done since being here, and I’m impressed with your work ethic. As you may know, Myers is steadily growing, and by the end of this quarter, there will be a need for more “talent” to groom into holding expanded responsibilities.”

Lauren paused so that the words took root in Janet’s mind. When she saw the small smile forming at the corners of her mouth, she continued,

“So, in a nutshell, I am planning to recommend that you have the chance to be one of the selected few to join our mentorship program. Everything going as I expect, you will be working directly with me. I want to be able to hand over some of my portfolios to someone I know is capable of doing an excellent job.”

“Thank you so much. I don’t know what else to say, but I promise not to let you down.”

“No need to promise me, promise yourself because

succeed or fail, it will be your career, not mine, that is affected. Also, stop letting others push you around. I know the team gives you more than your share of work. Start pushing back; you need to know how to stand your ground in a professional manner, of course," Lauren finished with a warm smile, wanting to show the young woman she was rooting for her.

"Thank you again for this opportunity, and yes, I will professionally deal with others as you recommend."

"Well, that's all for now. You can get back to work. I will let you know the moment the mentorship program enrollment has been approved," Lauren was standing now, stretching out her hand towards Janet.

Janet shook the hand upon rising, only to feel Lauren gently pull her to the left, slowly spinning her around. Taking her in from head to toe,

"When you start to work with me, you will need to dress the part more. I have a hairstylist I'll set you up with to give your hair a makeover. For the life of me, I don't know why you keep it tucked away in a bun all the time. If money is an issue, you'll be advanced the funds. This company has a thing about appearance when interacting with clients. Alright?"

"Ah, yes, of course. Thank you again," Janet said, trying not to touch her hair and straighten the blouse she was wearing over her skirt.

Lauren made her way to her office, happy to get started with the day. The meeting was not scheduled; it was just something that came about late last night after she got the distressing phone call from the CEO. Needless to say, she didn't sleep well with this newly added issue on her plate. Regardless, there was a job to be done, and everyone knows she has no problem shaking things up when needed. Lauren was well aware of the names she got called, but such things rolled off her back. *No one is paying my bills, and lined up to take the lead in my life. Besides, I worked hard to get where I am and really couldn't care less about office gossip and haters. If they only knew one kind word from me could have them right where they want to be. Just silly, when will people learn that hard work brings rewards?*

Her being 29 years old ruffled some feathers. In particular, those her age couldn't believe she got her position from work alone since the majority of the senior-level staff were much older. She'd just smile whenever she saw the expressions on their faces or heard the whispers about her modest office attire. What they still failed to realize is that Myers has clients from various industries, and being young and overly sexy in the office was not the image the company wanted to put out there. *Overtly sexy can get you only so far; competence is another story. Besides, I get sexy when it's called for.* As soon as her butt hit her office chair, Lauren's cell phone rang. The caller ID showed it was Marcus, her ex-boyfriend, who still wants to be friends. *Seriously!*

"Lauren, you are still coming to the wedding, right? Me and Tiffany are waiting for you to confirm your stay at the resort," Marcus' voice boomed in her ear, causing her to hold the phone several inches away.

"Yes, I am," she replied, rolling her eyes, wanting to slap herself for even getting sucked into this mess.

Marcus was getting married to Tiffany in just over a month, and she was invited after bumping into them at the mall one weekend. Lauren knew Marcus wanted to rub it in her face for ending things with him. He still, to this day, swears up and down he was faithful to her, despite the psycho girl Peaches showing up to Lauren's apartment with text messages, pictures, and a short cell phone video she has yet to erase from her memory.

The wedding was going to be "rustic" as Tiffany's family was big on the outdoors, so that pretty much dictated the venue. Lauren was not at all crazy about being out in nature; she was a city girl at heart. But she sucked it up and accepted the verbal invitation on the spot to save face. *No way is this fool going to break me ever again. I will smile my ass off while he latches onto this ...Tiffany. Sorry for her, but jumping the broom, it ain't me.* There were moments when the memories felt raw and fresh. Marcus was her first real boyfriend, and not even a year after they had broken up, he was getting married.

"Are you bringing a date? You know the suites sleep more than one person. I mean if you ain' got nobody, that's cool too. Tiffany just wanted to narrow down the headcount, that's all. Ahh, if you stuck, you know a lot of my boys would love to escort you," Marcus practically sang with certainty, the fishing intent evident in his tone.

"Yes, I have a date, Marcus. You can tell Tiffany it will be Lauren plus one. As a matter of fact, my boyfriend is quite excited about this mini vacation," She sang back, trying to sound as light and excited as possible, all the while twisting a sheet of paper from a folder on her desk.

Shit, where the hell am I going to find a boyfriend?

What did I let my pride get me into? Panic started to grip her chest, slowly tightening.

"Well, okay then. I'll catch up with you later." Marcus hurriedly hung up the phone. Her response had thrown him off his game. Realizing she had surprised him, Lauren chuckled to herself.

Staring out her office window at the city skyline, she racked her brain trying to think of who she could get to take as her date, correction "boyfriend." *I haven't even casually dated anyone since Marcus. My life has just been about work and forgetting his sorry ass. Arrrggg!*

Lauren barely noticed the faint knock at her office door. Her assistant Eli, soon after, walked in. A lock of dirty blonde hair had fallen out of place, resting just above his left eyebrow. He wore a crisp white button-down shirt and gray pants that fitted to his built frame. Undoubtedly, its matching jacket was hanging over the back of his desk chair. Well, moisturized light pink lips stretched into a quick smile,

"Hello, Ms. Shaw. I have your meeting folders for today. Also, I have your dinner on order; it's Italian."

Eli walked over to her desk, placing the folders neatly in a row along its side. She usually worked late and ordered dinner from nearby restaurants, especially since there was no one else at home to cook for. She looked at her assistant as if for the first time. Judging, he seemed to be about 5' 10" or so with light blue eyes and a well-toned body topped with a full head of multi-highlighted blond hair. The sight made Lauren swallow hard. She often wondered why an attractive man such as himself wanted to get into finance, stuck in an office all day long. He could easily make lots of money in front of a camera.

Eli had been her assistant for just over a year, coming in under the mentorship program. Mr. Richardson, his initial mentor, had retired, and Lauren was in need of help, so Eli happily volunteered. He was a pleasant kid, and they worked well together. *God, he sure doesn't look much of a kid, not like no kids she knew.* She knew he was younger than she was, but not quite sure just what his age was. *Maybe about 22 or 24 at the most. Hmm, I've got to find out now; curiosity suddenly has the best of me.* His face was now scrunched up, deep in thought.

"Ms. Shaw, do you mind if I borrow four hundred dollars?"

The question caught her off guard. With a raised eyebrow, she asked,

"And what would you use the money for?"

"Well, I had an emergency. Had some car trouble and spent more on repairs than calculated. As a result, my rent is about to be overdue."

Her initial instinct was to say no and offer to see if she could have payroll advance him the money, but then a win-win solution came to mind.

"Alright then."

"Really?" His face turned towards her, those blue pools shining, and his sexy lips stretched to show beautiful white teeth.

"Yes, really. There is one condition, though."

Eli tilted his head slightly, eyebrows raised with a questioning look on his face.

Chapter Two

Lauren

The time between "the boyfriend bargain," as I like to call it, and the pending due date of Marcus' wedding went by quickly. It was all hands on deck in the buzzing office. Everyone was playing a part in getting things ready for the follow-up meeting with Trident, Inc., leaving me with barely any time to dress shop for this blasted event. I still couldn't believe I was going. Regardless, I looked at it as a chance to shatter the image I was certain most of the people who'd be attending had of me, single and miserable. Either way, I plan to give them a whole lot to talk about. The beginning of the road of no return has arrived.

In another hour, Eli and I would be boarding the airplane. It had taken him a while to finally dismiss his apprehensions of being my "boyfriend" for this wedding. In the end, he went along with it, seeing that there were no other options to get the cash he needed for his rent. Having to touch me was something Eli kept bringing up. In his mind, I was the boss. So, to get him accustomed to being so close and affectionate, I had us practice being a couple at my apartment almost every evening. Trying it at the office when everyone had left proved not to work; it just made him freeze up even more.

It was the crack of dawn, and I hadn't had my usual cup of coffee yet. Grumpy is a kind way to describe my case of caffeine withdrawal. Deciding to travel comfortably, I wore a fitted t-shirt, yoga pants, and some running shoes; a lightweight jacket covered my handbag in the seat next to me in the airport terminal. My hair was braided to one side, with the end draped over the front of my left shoulder. Eli looked just as comfortable, but his sexy frame was no less evident in a pair of loose jeans, a polo shirt, and sneakers, a hoodie-style jacket casually draped over his toned right thigh. He was sitting next to me, fooling around with his cell phone. The busy sounds of the airport lulled me into a place where I was forced to deal with the mixed emotions and thoughts threatening to overwhelm me.

It had been taxing, trying to act as if I had gotten over Marcus so quickly. Our breakup ripped me to the core. I had trusted Marcus wholeheartedly, even dismissing the signs and subtle changes in him. My days were lived in a fantasy created by my stupid pride of wanting to have the perfect relationship, the perfect life. Never once did I stop to talk to him about things. I just acted like everything would take care of itself.

Once our relationship started to go downhill, I drowned myself in work. I didn't know how else to deal with his neglect and the widening distance between us. My mindset was that all I needed to do was keep him satisfied, help pay bills, take trips wherever he wanted to go, and have shopping sprees, and the like. To me, that's what we needed to stay together. Then, the truth hit all the life out of me; we had no real communication. The little we did have was all superficial, nothing really about a future together, family, and dreams. We always fought those last few months. All I did was work to push out the building heartache; all he did was hang out with friends, well, at least that's what I let myself believe. Then, when psycho chick showed up at my door, I lost it. *No use in reliving that nightmare over and over, girl. Now you know what to do, have them deep conversations. Get all the cards out on the table from the jump.*

Eli's hand gently shakes my right leg, snapping me back from my thoughts in time to hear our flight being called over the intercom. I gathered my things, trying not to drop my handbag as I wiggled into my jacket. The accidental brush of his fingers against my hand as he removed the now slipping handbag strap sent an electric jolt up my core. Trying hard to hide the blush on my face, I lowered my head only to remember my hair was pulled back in a braid and wouldn't be providing the curtain I desperately wanted at that moment. The only thing left to do was walk as if the act was nothing out of the ordinary between us.

Once settled in our seats, I closed my eyes, focusing on anything but the events soon to test my resolve. *Too late, Missy, you just got to suck it up!* Eli must have been watching me because the moment I let out a long exhale, I felt his warm breath tickling my right ear,

"Don't worry; I'll be with you every step of the way.

Besides, Marcus was a fool for thinking he could ever replace a woman like you."

With eyes still closed, I let Eli's words sink deep down my soul. Even though we were putting on a show, hearing the tenderness and sincerity in his voice brought on a slow smile; without a second thought, I leaned into him. His soft lips pressed now against my cheek, causing me to remain still longer than I wanted to. Well, more prolonged than I wanted him to see me hold it. *Girl, you need to keep your mind on the mission. All your sudden cravings and body acting on impulse are gonna get you in an even bigger predicament than you bargained for.* Frustrated again, I shifted in my chair, trying to get comfortable, and begged sleep to take me, if only for a little while.

Eli

I hated flying but dared not let Lauren know. She was a lifeline to me in my pretentious, sudden need for cash. She had passed the test. This prospect of playing her boyfriend was a pleasant bonus. Running my fingers through my hair, I glanced over at her to see that she was trying to sleep. It amazes me that people relax enough to sleep on airplanes. By this time, I would usually be starting to feel cramped and nervous about taking off. The more I watched Lauren, the more relaxed I became. She had shifted several times, finally keeping still once curled up, leaning only inches away from me.

In all the time I've worked with her, she's treated me more as a young boy than a man. The age difference never bothered me, but nothing I do seems to change her point of view. I was informed to always refer to her as Ms. Shaw from the first day I joined the company. Ms. Shaw, this and Ms. Shaw that, while I, on the other hand, was just Eli, never Mr. Sorensen. I've been more of a man than many who let their intentions for her show openly around the office, not to mention several of her portfolio clients.

Often, whenever I would catch them staring at her, raking her body from head to toe, I'd return a threatening glance. The men certainly didn't see me as a young boy. No, to them, I was Mr. Eli Sorensen. *Ahh, better try to keep things just how she wants them. Remember, this is all for show, and none of it means anything to her. No matter how much you want her, she'd never give you a shot. Forget that! If I get a chance to take things further on this trip or whenever I'm going for it.*

I slowly licked my lips, all while inhaling the sweet floral scent of her hair. By this time, she's slumped over the dividing armrest, head dangerously close to the now stiffening bulge in my pants. Pushing down the thought of her taking me right there and then in her wet mouth, I gently as possible, lifted her upper body and pushed the armrest all the way up. Still knocked out, I slowly rest Lauren's head on my lap, using my folded hoodie jacket as a pillow. Fixing herself again, she snuggled me, then became still as I mentally prepared myself for the airplane's take off; anything not to think of her soft lips on me.

Once in the air, I began to imagine what it could be like with this beautiful woman. She's so sexy and smart. There's humor, too. She thought I didn't recognize it, but I often overhear her chatting with friends on the phone and catch her quick comebacks in the office with other senior staff members. Every day, I wondered just what clothing would be caressing her tight body. Her legs were, more often than not, extending from under some variation of a skirt. Those legs I so wanted to run my hands up, exploring the unknown world between her thighs. And her ass, a thing of beauty, round and undeniable. Overall, she was heavier on the bottom, but that's just how I like it.

To my relief, they announced that we could use our electronic devices. Gladly, I reached for my cell phone to play a game of Sudoku. Anything was better than being tortured, watching Lauren sleep, not being able to touch her more than I already was. Still, occasionally, my eyes would scan down the length of her. Feeling her weight in my lap kept me excited whenever my mind drifted from the game. Some relief would eventually come as I focused on the current crushing the game was doing to me.

Yeah, definitely. Should that opportunity come, I will be making her moan and then scream my name. I'ma show her just how much of a young boy I'm not. She will learn to call me Mr. Sorensen, Mr. Eli Sorensen. Sweet sexy ass! Hmm, wait a minute, she never mentioned if I would be sleeping in a separate room. I mean, it would be suspicious if I did so……..HELL YEAH, one way or another, I will be learning the secret places of Lauren, I mean Ms. Shaw, this weekend! With a broad smile, I attack the game, knowing either way, I will be a winner in a short while.

Lauren

The pilot's announcement that we would be landing in 10 minutes stirred me from my slumber. I was a bit cramped, but at least my head was resting on something soft. Sudden panic took hold of me when I realized I was lying down, lying down on Eli's lap. His intoxicating smell of cologne was now all tangled in my nose hairs. His masculine scent danced with it, making my nipples hard and my hands itching to touch the abs pressing against his shirt a few inches from my face. As gracefully as I could manage, I sat up, smoothing my hair and stretching my twisted torso, hoping to realign my body.

"Thank you," I said to him as he just smiled and nodded his head before returning his attention to his phone.

Moments later, as I was reapplying my lipstick, the pilot announced that we were making our descent and everyone should be prepared for landing. Eli was now stretching before me, peeking out the tiny airplane's window. The ground below was approaching fast, and my nerves were returning right along with it. Unknowingly, I grabbed Eli's hand for reassurance. He gently rubbed my arm with his free hand.

Once we landed and were taxiing towards the gate, I stole a glance at him. In the past few days, he had suddenly seemed different to me. In my mind, I traced the strong line of his jaw. He looked….. mature, sexy. I swallowed hard as my mouth now longed to suck his lips.

I wonder if he knows how to use those. Is he a three-stroke and done type, or does he take his time and mix it up, rough then tender? Watching him now and remembering how skillfully he held me while we practiced being a couple, I'm hoping he is the latter.

The jolt of the airplane, as it stopped, brought me to the real world and away from a potentially dangerous fantasy. Glad for the distraction, I checked my makeup once again and mentally braced myself for the dreaded introductions with Marcus and his soon-to-be bride, Tiffany, not to mention the others sure to be in attendance.

Chapter Three

Lauren

I decided to let Eli drive the rental since he was "the man" in our relationship, and the more I let him take the lead, others may believe we were indeed a couple. He maneuvered the SUV around the resort's grounds, pulling up to the front door slowly as if wanting everyone to see our grand arrival.

I let out a groan, already spotting some of Marcus' family members making their way inside. Once the valet took the keys from Eli, he turned to me and said one word: wait. Not sure what he was about to do, I obliged and took a few deep breaths to compose myself. Eli had walked around to my side and opened the door.

Holding out a hand for me to take, he supported me as I climbed down the raised vehicle. This in itself caused some stares and knowing smiles from onlookers and the first of many "hellos."

"Lauren? Lauren Shaw, is that you?" Wendell, Marcus's cousin, practically shouted a few cars behind us, head stuck out the passenger side of the vehicle.

"And so, it begins," I said under my breath for only Eli to hear.

Following the voice, his eyes rested on Wendell, who was giving him a screwed-up face. Taking it as his cue, Eli closed the door behind me, snaking his arm around my waist, pulling me into his side. The hardness of his body next to mine felt like heaven. It had been a long time since a man held me this way in public. He led us towards the lobby doors and then turned so that Wendell would get the chance to see it was me, indeed.

"Lauren Shaw, I knew it was you! I told everybody I could spot you a mile away. Girl, you still lookin' good," Wendell said, all the while glaring up and down at Eli, who was still holding me tightly against his toned frame.

"Hey, Wendell, how have you been?" I replied while trying to loosen Eli's grip a little, squirming to break free.

It only made his hand pull me in more.

"Oh, yeah, you know, I been good. Moved back to the old hood since I got a new job nearby. Plus, you know, it's best to stay near family and not try to be outside your territory." The last remark I was certain he was throwing at Eli, but before I could say anything, I heard words that made me blush…. hard.

"I know just what you mean. That's why I stay guarding mine. You never know when someone might feel overconfident and want to challenge a man's boundaries. Hi, Eli Sorensen, Lauren's boyfriend."

I did my best not to laugh, seeing Wendell's jaw drop slightly at what Eli had said.

"Yeah, yeah, nice to meet you, man. Wendell, cousin of the groom."

With that, Eli spun us around and headed towards the registration desk. I could feel not only Wendell's gaze upon us but also those of several people in the lobby. By this time, the threat of hurling my guts out had come and gone. *Why the hell are you so nervous? You acting like you're the bride here. To hell with whatever people think or say. Hold your head up and strut next to this fine-ass man. But one thing you do not do is show that you got no other options since Marcus.*

"Welcome to The Lux Resort. How may I help you?" a young lady greeted us while flashing a bright smile.

"Thank you. I have reservations for two: Lauren Shaw."

"Alright, just give me a moment while I check you in."

I turned to Eli, giving him a grateful smile for the way he dealt with Wendell. He understood and bent down, planting a soft kiss on my forehead. The action was a bit surprising, but I soon understood why he did it. Within a few moments, Marcus approached.

"Well, so glad you could make it. I see you managed to bring a guest."

"Hello, Marcus, and as I promised, I came. I didn't have to manage anything; this is my boyfriend, Eli. Marcus Hillert, Eli Sorensen."

"Nice to finally meet you, Eli. Lauren hasn't told me much about you."

"I can't imagine she would, since she's only been communicating with you over recent weeks. Besides, she has me. Why would she still need to discuss anything with an ex?"

Marcus's jaw went tight, but his eyes still pretended to smile. Eli stood his ground. By now, he'd taken hold of my left hand. Not wanting to appear defeated, Marcus replied,

"Well, I guess you're right. I sure wouldn't want my wife to be spending time with her ex. Speaking of which, let me introduce you to my lovely bride-to-be. Tiffany, sweetheart, there are some people I want you to meet."

A slim young woman approached us after breaking free from a small group of people several feet away. She was beautiful, if I had to be honest. Her hair was different than the first time we met in the mall when I let myself be suckered into attending this event. She now wore it straight, falling just short of her shoulders. Standing near Eli, I could easily see them both doing a fashion spread in any magazine. Her skin was smooth and radiated the color of nutmeg. The natural light now flooding the lobby did it more justice than the fluorescent bulbs of the mall. Dark brown eyes glimmered with the excitement of the upcoming nuptials. Woman to woman, I honestly couldn't be happier for her. Hopefully, their relationship was built on a stronger foundation than Marcus and I.

"Dear, you remember Lauren, and this is Eli

Sorensen, her boyfriend." Marcus' voice ended on a note of unbelief about the real relationship between Eli and I.

"Hello, Tiffany, nice to see you again. I must say this place looks like the ideal wedding spot," I beam, trying to squash the building tension between the men.

"Hi, and thanks so much for coming. Yes, there are so many lovely areas around the property. Hello Eli, thanks also for coming to share this wonderful occasion with us. Hmm, your face seems familiar. Have we met before?"

"No, I'm certain to have remembered," Eli smiled, extending a hand toward Tiffany. Shaking it, he added, "You may have seen my photo during my brief modeling days."

"Ahh, yes, that's it. You were the face and body," Tiffany blushed, "for Top Alps-Letics."

"Good memory."

"So, whatever happened? You stopped modeling?"

"I put it on hold," Eli grinned, now removing his hand from mine and returning it to my waist, causing sensations to spark in unmentionable places.

"Well, Lauren, looks like you've got yourself a celebrity," Marcus practically snickered. "You better keep a close eye on him before the fans snatch him away.”

“Oh, she does not need to worry about that. She’s all the woman a man could ever need and hope for.”

The sudden deafening silence that engulfed us was broken by the cheery voice of the lady from behind the registration desk.

“Excuse me, Ms. Shaw, your room is ready.”

“Well, I need a nap before this evening’s festivities start. We’ll see you both later,” I blurted out before turning to collect the room keys.

With his arm still wrapped around my waist, Eli waved his free hand toward the bride and groom while guiding me toward the elevators. Marcus was still wearing an expression of disdain.

“That went well. I’m proud of you, Lauren. Not once did your voice waver, and I must say it was rather fun watching Marcus’ reactions. I think I will most definitely enjoy our stay here.”

“Thanks, but don’t make him too upset that it ruins things for Tiffany. Every bride wants the perfect wedding, and though Marcus will always be an ass to me, this means a lot to her. Say whatever, but as a woman *someday*, I look forward to that perfect wedding, too.”

Eli

So that was Marcus, huh? Yeah, this trip is going to be a lot of fun. He definitely hasn't gotten over Lauren as well as he'd like everyone to think. Too bad, she's now fair game, and I intend to claim her for myself.

Upon opening the door to our suite, I quickly tipped the porter and headed to the balcony. The view was a sweet change from the concrete jungle I saw every day. There was a large forested area in the distance. Between it and the resort, the grounds were a maze of flower beds, an actual mini-maze, miniature golf, several swimming pools, and larger grassed areas. One was currently being decorated and appeared to be where the wedding would take place the following afternoon. The sound of the bathroom door closing and the forceful water of the shower let me know Lauren was getting ready for her nap. I figured it would be a good time to check out the bedroom.

Just around a half wall was a giant, somewhat comfortable-looking king-sized bed. Not seeing any cot or pullout, I could only assume we'd be sharing it. I took off my footwear and socks and pulled out a pair of shorts to change into once Lauren was out of the shower.

It wasn't long before she emerged, hair now loose framing her face while a tank top and shorts hugged the curves that made her Ms. Shaw! Trying not to stare, I grabbed my toiletries bag and headed for the bathroom.

"And don't be leaving the toilet seat up, please, and thank you. God knows I don't want to fall into that thing in the middle of the night half asleep."

"Yes, dear," I replied, chuckling to myself.

Closing the door, the scent of her shower gel accosted my nose. A wicked smile crept across my face as thoughts of her warm skin against my lips came to mind. Shaking them away, I stood under the stream of warm water, only to be seized by a vision of her enjoying the pounding of it with me. Her wet curls hanging down her back, hard nipples begging me to ease their pain. The sudden rush of blood between my thighs made me groan in frustration. *Soon, buddy, just hold on a little longer. I promise you will explore her hidden treasure real soon.*

When I got out of the bathroom, Lauren was already fast asleep. She didn't even pull back the covers, just flat on her stomach, sprawled almost dead center in the bed. It was all I could do not to lay on top of her, gently stroking her from behind. Deciding to just join her in taking advantage of the few hours before the evening's meet and greet, I eased onto the bed, trying not to get too close, tucking one of the many pillows under my head. I don't know how long I gazed at her sleeping face before I, too, was knocked out.

The weight and sudden jerk of something on my right thigh pulled me from sweet slumber. Lauren had tossed in her sleep and was now laying on her back, legs spread open, left one on my right. I almost didn't breathe as I slowly turned my head to see if she was still asleep, out cold. Before I could ease her off of me, she turned, this time scissoring me with her legs. My left leg was stuck under her weight. Breasts were now pressed up against my right arm, and the warmth of her breath tickled my neck. Closing my eyes and exhaling slowly, I tried to figure out just how to break free. Coming up with nothing, I decided to nudge her off gently. Such action proved only to do more harm than good.

"Umm baby, not yet. Let's stay in bed just a little longer. You know how I love to snuggle," she moaned, still fast asleep.

Then, her hand reached my crotch, and she slowly rubbed the thin fabric that separated our skins. Swallowing hard, I then whispered,

"Lauren, wake up. Lauren dear, you're dreaming, wake up."

"Umm, you feel so good, and I can tell you don't want to get up either. Someone wants me to play with them!"

"Lauren….Lauren. Ms. Shaw!" I finally said just loud enough to make her eyes snap open in shock and a glimpse of horror.

"What….what the?"

"You were dreaming. I tried to push you off, but you just locked onto me," I said with a gentle smile. "It's okay, nothing out of the way happened."

"Then why is my hand on your…oh my God," she said, snatching her hand from my now almost complete erection.

"No worries. You can't expect a man not to be turned on by someone so sweet and beautiful as yourself, now can you?"

"You are not some man. You're…"

"I'm Eli, your boyfriend. And just like you've been

saying, we need to act more naturally around each other if anyone is going to believe we're dating. Hmm, no, I think you want them to see us as madly in love, correct?"

"Well, I mean…"

"You mean, yes, as in madly in love."

With that, I leaned into her, gently brushing my lips against hers. I pulled away slightly, only to adjust myself, and then parted her lips with my eager tongue. She hesitated, not sure whether to allow me in or not. It was all the time I needed, though, to own her sweetness. Before she knew what was happening, she was already drowning in my touch. Hardening nipples and the slow movement of her hips confirmed it.

Chapter Four

Lauren

"You should start getting dressed. I think I'll go downstairs and grab a snack from one of the eateries in the lobby. Would you like for me to bring you back something?" Eli offered as he pulled away from me, sitting with legs swung over the side of the bed.

My mind was still trying to sort out what had just happened. Eli said nothing did, but my hand on his hardening erection was not what I would consider nothing. And that kiss! I'm just too emotional right now, and using him for some relational comeback is not what I want at all. Still, he has started to get under my skin.

"I don't know if I can eat at the moment. Butterflies are returning to my stomach."

"Well, if I see anything I think you'll like, I'll be sure to bring it back. So, what, we will be leaving in another hour and a half or so?"

"Yeah, about around that time."

"Cool. See you in a few."

With that, he pulled on a polo shirt and a pair of sneakers and was out the door.

When finally arriving downstairs, they headed towards the back patio area where the festivities had already begun. Glad for the cover of the night and the obvious effect the endless pouring of alcohol was having on many of the guests, Lauren did her best to stay on the perimeter. She honestly didn't want to interact with anyone. Being the groom's ex-girlfriend was branding enough, and having to act like this all was no big deal had already taxed her nerves. Sensing her growing anxiety, Eli decided to lead them to a side table of hors-d'oeuvres and a large punch bowl. While Lauren glanced around the area, he filled two small plates with food and handed them to her. Upon filling two glasses with the punch, he motioned to an empty bench just off in the grass.

"Try to eat something. It wouldn't be pretty having you faint in front of everyone, now would it?"

"No, it wouldn't."

They sat in silence while enjoying the food assortment. Lauren pretended to be totally consumed by the act of eating, not wanting to gaze about, afraid she'd lock eyes with several of the questioning faces. Eli, on the other hand, scanned the attendants, mentally noting many of the expressions and curious glances they both got, him in particular.

Marcus had noticed their arrival and was doing his best to stay planted next to Tiffany as they slowly made their rounds, thanking each guest for attending. He didn't miss how attentive Eli was to Lauren and that she appeared to cling to him for support. Her showing up was quite a shock as he would never have wagered she would follow up on his dare of an invitation to come to his wedding, not after the way things ended between them.

Still, he had found Tiffany, and she was a great catch, but with the innocence Lauren had when they first met, he wished he would have found another. This time, though, he knew much better just how to love and mold his woman. Turning to Tiffany, Marcus reached for her waist and gave a gentle squeeze. In the end, she was the one who made him realize just how much he lost with Lauren when she threatened to leave him, too. That made him get his act together and not let another opportunity at real love pass him by.

Taking one more side glance at Lauren and Eli, he caught the back rubbing he was giving her and the reassuring smile. He knew Lauren was not comfortable being there, and now he wished his dumb ego hadn't put her on the spot, asking her to attend. *That was a real bitch move, Marcus!* Sighing, he excused himself and Tiffany from the guests they were talking with and headed toward Lauren and Eli; might as well get it over with. *I'm sure she's only hanging out long enough to make a short appearance before getting lost somewhere else.*

"Hello, lovely people. You look well-rested, Lauren," Marcus said, genuinely meaning it. He was still mentally kicking himself for inviting her.

"Hello to the future Mr. and Mrs. Hillert," replied Eli with a beaming smile, "you picked a beautiful place for your special occasion, and we are happy to be here. Isn't that right, Dear?"

"Yes," Lauren managed to get out after feeling the gentle pressure of Eli's arm now wrapped around her shoulders, steadying her on the bench.

"Well, again, Lauren, I just wanted you to know how much we both appreciate you being here and do enjoy the resort's many amenities."

"They have many lovely spots around the grounds. Perfect for relaxing under the stars," Tiffany added while giving a wink to Eli.

"I shall have to put that to the test then," Eli replied, shooting Lauren a bright smile.

"Well, we still have several guests to greet, so we'll leave you two alone. Have fun," Marcus said as he pulled on Tiffany's hand, walking away.

"You okay?"

"Yes, thanks. Glad that's done and so ready to go explore anywhere but here."

"Then let's see if Tiffany gave us good intel on this place," Eli said, taking their plates and glasses and setting them on a nearby table.

They wandered along the path that ended with the opening of the maze, formed of lush green foliage. Not caring which direction they went, Lauren aimlessly followed Eli into the private oasis. After a few twists and turns, Lauren asked if he had any idea how to get out.

"Well, my dear, that's the whole point. Get lost until you do."

"Great! These shoes are starting to hurt my feet, and you decide to get us lost in a freaking maze. Why the hell did I even follow you in here?"

"Because you were desperate to be invisible from all the curious eyes back there. Or maybe because you wanted to be alone with me again, hmm?"

By this time, Eli had them facing a dead end and turned to Lauren, slowly walking towards her with a devilish grin creeping across his beautiful face.

"Don't come near me."

The space between them only shortened with every step Eli took. His blue orbs, now with specks of silver shimmering in the moonlight, raked shamelessly up and down her body. His grin had turned into a smirk once he saw the apprehension on Laurens' face.

"What's wrong, my sweetness? I thought you liked it when we played lovers?"

"There's no one around, so no need to "play lovers"

at the moment."

"But who said I was playing?" By now, Eli was only one step away from having his body pressed against hers.

His skin appeared creamy in the night light. The contrast of the sky and the maze behind him was putting her in a trance. The scent of him was stirring feelings from not so long ago. *What did he mean by not playing? They had an agreement...right?*

"What did you mean by not playing? We have an agreement, remember?"

"I remember the agreement. I also know there was nothing about it remaining a charade. There are no clauses about things becoming serious and real between us."

"You forget your place, Eli. I am your boss, and in exchange for the agreed amount you needed, you would pretend to be my boyfriend for this wedding."

"My place? Seems to me the more I get to know you, the clearer "my place" becomes," Eli whispered now as his body finally made contact with hers. "Besides, your actions have been consistent in pointing out just where "my place" is, and it's not just as your assistant."

"I don't know what you think is going on here, Eli, but we are sticking to the agreement. I'll admit, things did get personal a bit, and I took advantage of your touch in a moment of weakness."

"Oh, is that what you call it?" He laughed, leaning closer to her face.

Lauren

I could feel his warm breath on my face now. The nearness of him was starting to make me light-headed; moisture was building fast as I did my best to squeeze myself so none would escape me. As I took a slight step back from the oncoming threat of a kiss, my shoe heel got caught in the grass; I felt myself falling. Before fully registering what was happening, a strong arm braced me, crashing my breast into firm chest muscles. Our eyes became fixed on each other, and it took all I had to snap myself to my senses.

"Let go of me," I demanded, pushing now against his shoulder with no effect.

"Not until you admit you have feelings for me. That you want us to be more than what we are."

"Have you lost your mind? We work together, nothing more. Try to stick to the plan and not get confused between acting and reality."

"Oh, I'm not the one confused here. I very well know the difference when it comes to you." Without another word, Eli took my mouth.

He kissed me hard, and the moment I parted my lips to protest, his tongue searched for mine. Futilely, I tried to resist, squirming and twisting my head, but his free hand planted me still. Seeing it was pointless to deny I liked it, I let him continue as my body slowly relaxed in his arms. His taste was sweet, and the memory of his fingers working their magic on my back from before only set off another ignition of flame and moisture between my legs. When I began reaching for him, he pulled away.

Without a word, he grabbed my hand and led us back out of the maze. It's obvious he was pretending to be lost, as he didn't hesitate at each turn. Before long, we were again passing through the entrance of the maze, making a bee-line for a side entrance to the lobby, away from the wedding guests.

The elevator ride was quiet. I didn't know what Eli was thinking, and my emotions were just everywhere. I can't deny I was falling for his charms, but charms were not enough. Then there's the fact that I'm his boss. What about work? How are we supposed to fix that issue? He'd have to transfer to another team. Shit, this is getting too complicated, and all because of damn Marcus!

Once the door of the suite was closed, Eli turned to face me. The moonlight had the room light up beautifully, casting shadows near the corners.

"You need to make up your mind, Lauren, about just what you want?"

"What I want?"

"Yes, your wants. Think about it; really think about it. Let's not kid ourselves. For a long time, there has been an undercurrent between us. From the first day I saw you when I started at the firm, you had my nose wide open. I never said or did anything about it because, frankly, I wasn't sure if you had the slightest interest in me."

"All that time you were attracted me?"

"Attracted, then consumed," Eli said, coming closer to me. "If working together is what concerns you, then don't. I was planning on telling you when we got back home, but now is as good a time as any.

"Tell me what?" I asked, desire now replaced by apprehension.

"I never needed the money. It was just a test."

"A test. I don't understand."

"As Tiffany mentioned, I had quite a successful modeling career before working at Myers. The money I saved was invested in several companies, and the dividends have finally started to roll in. Also, Myers provided the experience I wanted in understanding finance for my future business deals."

I just stood there stunned. Here, I thought this young man was struggling and needed my help to make ends meet. All the while, he was playing me. Heat began to crawl up the sides of my face as anger took hold.

"Exactly what kind of test were you conducting on me, Eli? I thought you were in a tight spot and needed help. Now you tell me you're practically rich, and I was some lab rat to satisfy what test exactly?"

"I wanted, no needed, to be sure you had no financial ambitions towards me."

"Financial ambitions? Alright, you have me lost here."

"Months ago, I had made up my mind to ask you out once I had resigned, of course. Before revealing too much about myself, I decided to see if you were like many other women I've come across, only wanting me for my money.

If you saw me as poor and still went out with me, I'd have a more meaningful clue as to the type of woman you are."

"So if I had said no, you were going to assume I was what, a gold digger?"

"I wouldn't call you a gold digger, but because you haven't been seen with anyone, I had to start somewhere. So, I started with money, then I was going to see if maybe you preferred only black men, leaving me out of the running."

I just stared at him, not knowing now what to think or feel. My head was spinning as I tried to put all the pieces together. Brief memories of his interactions with me came to mind, his always smiling face. Sweet, thoughtful gestures and attention to detail, all of which I thought were just him being an efficient assistant. Shit!

"Eli, I…"

"Shhh, it's a lot to take in, I know. This is not how I planned it to happen, but I wanted you to know all the facts before you make another decision regarding me, regarding us." He reached again for me, only this time, he walked me to the dressing area before turning away.

"I'll let you change your clothes and get some rest. Tomorrow will be another interesting day, and I want to let you know I will continue to hold up my end of the agreement for the wedding ceremony. I'll sleep on the sofa tonight."

With that, I was left alone in the dark space. Soft moonlight streaked across the bed that now appeared too large just for me to sleep on. My mind was a full-blown tornado of thoughts. My body wanted his touch; my heart was refusing to melt the ice casing Marcus had left behind. *Maybe a good hot shower will help me relax and sort out some of these conflicting emotions and thoughts I'm having.*

The fire that was burning between my legs, though, was still not completely out. The urge to just throw everything out the window and have one reckless, hot night of lovemaking with a fine-ass man threatened to overtake me again. Squeezing my eyes shut, I forced myself to think of nothing but the upcoming wedding and why I was here. That did the trick almost instantly.

Chapter Five

A rustling sound woke Lauren from a deep sleep. She had been dreaming about a mixture of things, but one memory remained fresh as she propped herself up in the bed, trying to discern what the noise was. Remembering where she was, Lauren let out the held breath, trying to focus her eyes in the moonlit room. Eli had left the sliding door to the balcony open, allowing the tranquil sounds of nature to flow into the suite.

Deciding to close the door, Lauren tiptoed around the bed, doing her best not to wake him, only to find he was not on the sofa. Bathing in the moonlight, Eli was stretched in a chair, head tilted back with his frame extended as if sunbathing. The sight of him made Lauren gasp since all that covered him was a thick white bath towel around his waist. Gently, she touched his shoulder to try to stir him.

"Hmm."

"Why are you sleeping out here? Are you trying to get sick from exposure?"

"I just got here, and no, I plan to be in tip-top shape for the remainder of this trip," Eli said, slowly opening his eyes and drinking in the sexy tossed hair vision next to him.

Without a word, he reached for her hand and pulled her onto his lap. It took Lauren by surprise, causing her to brace herself against his frame so as not to end up on the ground.

"Ahh," she shrieked before his sculpted chest muffled her sounds against her lips. Eli's scent began to make her tongue twirl in her mouth. Deciding to press her lips together tightly, Lauren managed to balance on top of Eli, looking him dead in the eyes,

"Just what do you think you're doing? I came to see what the noise was I heard, then find you out here practically naked…"

"So, you do care about me, huh?"

"Of course, I care about you, silly. I need you to see me through this mess."

"I see. Then why are your nipples hard as pebbles? Could it be your body wants me, but your mind is cock-blocking?"

"How dare you speak to me that way?"

"I'm your boyfriend, remember? I can say and do with you whatever I want."

Before Lauren could shoot back a retort, Eli sat up and took her soft lips with his hot mouth. She had driven him crazy since the moment he saw her at the airport in those painted-on yoga pants. The airplane ride was the second cut she gave him. The third was in the maze just a while ago, and now, under the night sky, she dared challenge his manhood again. Lauren resisted only for a minute, finally succumbing to the heat which had never left since earlier.

She let herself feel his touch, moving as he did back into the suite. With the sliding door firmly shut behind them, Eli broke the kiss and sat on the sofa. Lauren stood unsure of what to do next. Seeing her confusion, Eli leaned back, stretching his legs,

"Your move."

"My move? Look, I admit something is happening between us, but you're my assistant, and I don't need any complications in my life right now."

"You forget, Lauren, that I'm no longer your assistant; well, at least technically, that won't be the case when we get back home. So, what do you want from me?"

Trying to push all the dirty things she wanted from the gorgeous display just a few feet away, Lauren shook her head and squared her shoulders,

"I want…"

"Yes?" Eli prodded while remaining completely stretched before her on the sofa.

"What do I want? I want to get through this travesty of my current life. Just want to put Marcus and my past behind me. I'm just tired of always having to be the perfect person. I want my life the way it was before I came here. That's what I want."

"So, what you want is to return to a life of work, take-out dinners, no social life or real friends. Did I miss anything? Oh, wait, and continue to build that wall around yourself so no one has any chance of ever getting close to you."

"Look, Eli, I want nothing more than to get through tomorrow and then return home. Since you feel the need to keep making it clear, you will no longer be my assistant.

What you do after that is your business. I really don't care."

"You don't care about me. Is that what you're saying, Lauren? You don't care. Okay, fine. A deal is a deal, and we made a bargain. I will play the perfect boyfriend, having all the women wishing they were you and all the men wishing they had you. We'll get through this, and when we get back home, we'll just go our separate ways. Okay?"

"Deal," Lauren scoffed, folding her arms across her chest while lifting her chin up a few inches.

"Deal!" Eli returned, but his reply was laced with disappointment, something Lauren caught, and it only confused her more as to what game he was indeed playing.

Before she had a chance to say anything further, Eli stood, which resulted in the towel almost exposing him fully. Lauren's eyes widened, seeing the towel nearly slip and finding she could not look away.

Instead, her tongue instinctively licked her lips, with her teeth tugging at her bottom one. With everything she did, Eli caught it and smiled just a little, returning a wanting gaze before heading to the bedroom area. Lauren followed a few minutes later to find he was tucked in under the covers, lying on his stomach.

"I thought you were taking the sofa?"

"I changed my mind. Besides, this bed is more than big enough for both of us. Good night."

Making a note to stay as close to the edge on her side, Lauren pulled back the covers just a bit too much, revealing a sculpted butt of creamy flesh.

"Yeah, I sleep in the nude."

"Not on this trip, you don't!"

"There was nothing outlined in the bargain to state otherwise. I read the fine print. Sweet dreams, my dear."

Seeing she was not going to win this battle, Lauren closed her eyes and let out a long sigh. Moisture was now wetting her panties for the millionth time tonight. She managed to find a comfortable position on her back with her head facing opposite of Eli. *This night is going to be a long one. Shit, shit, shit. And why am I so horny lately?*

It was about another hour before Lauren was able to drift off to sleep. This time, she was dreaming of walking alone on a beach. Ahead of her was a man, but she couldn't recognize who it was. No matter how fast she walked, they remained just out of reach. She then started to trot, only to end up in a full sprint; still, the man remained out of reach.

Tired and panting to catch her breath, she dropped to her knees, crying from a sudden flood of emotional dread. *Why can't I reach him? Will I always be alone?*

When she looked up again, the man was standing in front of her. She reached out and trailed his legs with her hands. His skin was cool to the touch. Then she felt her arms circle his waist, kneading his toned back muscles with her fingers. He was shirtless, and the feel of him made her let go of all fear and control. Her mouth found his abs, then his chest. Moaning escaped her lips as she feasted on him. Seconds later, they were joined by sounds from this mystery god. She heard her name being softly spoken as she continued to kiss, suck, and nibble sweet-tasting flesh.

"Lauren. Umm, ahhhh. Lauren, what are you doing? Ummm. If you don't stop, I won't be able to hold myself back. Lauren!"

The last call of her name made her open her eyes wide enough to see she was now hovering over Eli, who had long rolled on his back. Something throbbed against her torso. His scent tickled her nose.

"I was dreaming. Ahh, I was dreaming, right?"

"You were, but whatever you were doing in the

dream, you were doing in real life to me. I'm not complaining, but I wanted you to be fully aware of…..well, you know."

Eyes fully focused now, Lauren stared back at Eli, daring not to let her gaze go lower than his lips.

"I'm fine with this if you are. I'd never want you to do anything you don't want," He said softly, pushing back some of her loose hair.

His touch only stirred the heat Lauren was losing a grip over. Tired of being denied happiness and pleasure, she rubbed her head against his arm. Taking the cue to proceed, Eli gently pulled her down to him. He kissed her softly, then harder, until she pulled away and took up where she left off, discovering every inch of him.

Eli spread his legs so she had full access, watching her use her hands and mouth on him, causing his eyes to roll back. He trembled as her fingernails gently scraped his flesh, and needing to slow his arousal, he reached up and pulled her in again for a kiss. Flipping her this time on her back, he returned the favor, having her claw at the bedsheet and trying to muffle the screams with her hands.

They went at each other for some time into the early morning hours, holding each other tight, riding the waves of ecstasy. Finally, they gave in to exhaustion with enough time for them to get about five hours of sleep before the wedding began.

Chapter Six

To say the sight of them as they took their seats amongst the other guests went unnoticed is an understatement. Women visibly fanned themselves.

When Eli passed by. He looked like he'd just stepped off a runway at New York Fashion Week. The suit he wore was one of charcoal pants and a light grey jacket, both custom-fitted. The trail of cologne he left behind only reminded everyone he'd once been nearby. Lauren had managed to find a dress that accentuated her breasts and waist, with a long slit up the left side in a skirt of gathered, flowing fabric. The light grayish-silver color complemented Eli's suit beautifully. She appreciated that he dressed to match her once he saw the dress arrive at the office. It was such little details she'd always admired about him.

Neither had mentioned what had transpired only hours before. They dressed in almost complete silence, save for the pleasantries, while eating the light breakfast ordered through room service. Again, something Lauren appreciated about him. He gave her the space to deal with all that was going on with her, and if what they did was a one-time thing, he'd live with it for a while. He knew it would be great, yet he understood it could be so much more if she'd just break her wall down. Still, he was satisfied for the moment to at least be there with her. At least for the next day, she was all his.

They were approaching their seats, and Eli noted the glares from several of the guests. Deciding to give them a good show, he circled his arm around Laurens' waist.

"Again, you look amazing," he breathed against her ear, sending an electric shock wave down her back, holding her steady when he felt her flinch. "And yes, they're all looking at us. Just keep smiling."

Lauren was grateful for the chair that now supported her legs, which had lost their ability to keep her standing. Her hands were white-knuckled, clenching a small handbag as she thought of how she'd planned to one day be the bride at such an event. Seeing her smile start to fade,

Eli freed her bag from her hands and took one into his, gently stroking it with his fingers.

Feeling her relax, he focused on the groom, who was now walking along the aisle towards the altar. Of all the eyes Marcus could land on, they found Eli's. A silent exchange was made between the two men, and to Eli's surprise, Marcus gave a slight nod. Lauren turned her head just in time to see Eli nod back.

"What was that all about?"

"A truce. Marcus knows you are lost to him and that I have no intention of letting you go. Now smile, dear; you have much to be thankful for."

Deciding it was not the place to get into it with him, Lauren turned to face the front. Mentally, she took herself far away from there and thought of how life would now be different since she and Eli took that next step. *What next step? This is all pretend, remember. Forget what he said about not acting, he just wanted the goodies, and your hot ass gave it to him without the silver platter. Ahhh, just enjoy the fact that you got a good pounding and sampled some Grade-A meat before heading back to a life of celibacy. Yeah, celibacy 'cause you know ain' no man waiting for you back home.*

Tiffany made a beautiful bride. Once she started to walk down the aisle, Lauren's mind tuned everything out. When she was focused again, the newlyweds were down the aisle, being hugged by family and guests before walking off to take photos. Lauren had remained seated until they had walked off, happy for Eli to guide her to a nearby table of refreshments. She held onto his arm for dear life.

"Thank you for being here with me. I wouldn't have been able to take this alone."

"Even if we didn't make the bargain, I wouldn't have let you face this by yourself. Come, let's explore the flower bed for a moment. I think we could both use some time away from the oglers."

Standing in the midst of a wide variety of potted flowers, Eli watched Lauren begin to relax and enjoy their beauty.

"I think I'd like to start having some flowers delivered to my office on a weekly basis. They brighten any mood. Make sure to set that up when we get back, okay?"

"I would, but I'll no longer work for you, remember? But, I can personally deliver them if you want, along with a hand-written note explaining all the things I'd be doing with you each weeknight."

Spinning around to see his face was serious, Lauren smiled and shook her head before walking over to a small fountain nearby.

"When you're ready, we can talk about it or not."

"What's there to talk about? We're both adults and shared a wonderful night and early morning of great lovemaking."

"I wouldn't call what we did entirely lovemaking, Lauren. But I'd love to give that a go, too."

"I bet you would."

"Don't try and act like you're not interested. I have the bite and scratch marks to prove that you are; on my ass, for starters."

Blushing, Lauren nodded towards the tent set up for the reception, and Eli took her arm and led the way. As expected, there were whispers and stares, but once seated, they both made the most of the award situation. Thankfully, the bride and groom were kept busy entertaining others as well as being entertained that Lauren and Eli were able to slip away after eating their meal.

"Don't you want to say goodbye to them?"

"Not really. I've had enough of these people and would like to get out of here."

"I do believe we have one more night booked, don't we?"

"I have no problem leaving early and paying the penalty to change our flight. Why do you want to stay?"

"I mean, since we're here, we may as well enjoy it. How about a drive? We could go see the sights and be free of this crowd."

"Sure, that sounds better than having to wear a smile plastered across my face all afternoon."

With that, they went back to their suite to change into more comfortable clothes. Within the hour, they were driving along the highway toward a lookout spot the hotel concierge had recommended. The fresh breeze blowing through the SUV's window helped Lauren to relax more. She was happy to get away from the city for a while, and God knows she needed the vacation. Sadness, though, crept in a little as the reality of losing Eli around the office set in.

"Have you thought of my replacement yet?"

"Not really. I'm still waiting for you to tell me it was

all a joke."

"No joke. I think you should consider Janet. She's bright, pleasant, and hard-working. No, Eli, but she'll manage."

"Hmm, you may be right. Since I'll need someone right away, Janet would be a good choice."

"I'll be sure to show her how you like things done. As for dinners, I was hoping you'd have them with me."

"Oh, you do, do you?"

"What, you don't like eating with me? I'm great company and can hold dinner conversation with the best of them."

"This I know. I'm just not expecting you to keep up the act once we get back, remember?"

"You keep insisting that I'm acting."

"You got the "bonus" you hoped for. Let's just say our arrangement is concluded once the airplane lands in the city."

"If that's what you want."

"Yes, that's what I want Eli."

The SUV came to a stop just near the edge of a cliff. The view was something to see. Lauren had never seen anything like it and was silenced by its beauty. Eli got out and then helped her out as well. They stopped at the guardrail and enjoyed the moment.

"Being with you was never a 'bonus' as you put it. I only followed your lead and want to be with you if it's something you're comfortable with, something you want."

"I can't take another heartache, Eli. Besides, you can have any young woman you want. You don't need me."

"This is true; I mean, having any young woman I want part. But that is not what I want. Why do you feel as if you're not good enough? You're intelligent, beautiful, funny, sexy as hell, smell good, taste better, and make me hot at just the thought of you."

Lauren was now staring at him, half in surprise at his confession. She didn't really know how he saw her. He masked his feelings well all this time.

"Lauren Shaw, I can make you happy. I know you've had a bad experience with Marcus, but I'm not him. I see your value. I want, no, I need you in my life."

"Why? Why do you need me, Eli?"

"Because you're someone I can trust. Younger women or older, for that fact, will see my money and status first. They won't take the time to get to know me, not like you have. Won't you take a chance at being happy with me?"

Lauren exhaled long and hard. She couldn't deny he made her feel like royalty and that she longed to have the security of a relationship. Seeing Marcus get married was the final tug at the Band-Aid she'd used to cover the hole in her soul. She wanted to be complete again.

"I won't give away my heart so easily, not again. Sorry, I just can't do that. Any man that wants me will have to earn me."

"I can do knight and shining armor if that's what it takes," Eli whispered as he pulled her against him. "I also have access to a flower bed and endless chocolate, if that would make you happy too?"

"The flowers would be lovely, but not too much chocolate unless drizzled over you."

"Not a problem. I know you have a thing for eating me. Melted chocolate it is."

By now, he had his fingers lifting her chin, going in for a quick taste of her lips.

"I will make you forget all the hurt and pain. I promise to only bring you happiness and pleasure to the point you learn to scream my name."

"I think I already did."

"Ahhh, no, my dear. I plan to make you scream, Mr. Eli Sorensen."

"I see, and just how do you plan on accomplishing that?"

Without a word, Eli took her back to the SUV. He drove off about half a mile down the highway, turning off onto a dirt road he'd spotted on the way there. Parking between a pair of trees, he helped her into the back seat.

Without a word, he undressed her, then himself. With her straddling him, he took her without mercy. Steam began to fog the windows as he worked her wet delight with his manhood and kissed her lips until they were bruised.

With the rear seats fully reclined, he positioned her so he could claim her from behind. The depths he was able to reach made Lauren groan louder, causing her legs to shake from pleasure.

"What's my name?" Eli commanded, and he pulled her head back, creating a deeper arch in her back.

"Eli."

"No, what's my name?" This time, Eli was pounding her so hard the vehicle was rocking.

"Eli," Lauren managed to whisper through the silent

screams.

Waiting until she was almost ready to climax, Eli withdrew and kept still. Frantically, Lauren reached for him, but he spanked her hand away.

"Don't stop. What are you doing?" She begged.

Smacking her ass hard, leaving his handprint Eli asked again, this time in a tone that not only got her attention but made her juices run down her legs.

"WHAT'S MY NAME?"

"Eli Sorensen." His other hand smacked her other ass cheek, harder this time.

"Mr. Sorensen." Seeing him raise his hand to smack her ass again, she quickly corrected herself,

"Mr. Eli Sorensen."

"SAY IT AGAIN."

"Mr. Eli Sorensen."

Putting just his throbbing head to her opening, he commanded,

"AGAIN."

"Mr. Eli Sorensen."

"Now, what do you want from me?"

"Everything," Lauren said as she tried to hold back the tears brought on by both the stinging pain his hands had caused and the pleasure she was about to receive.

Without warning, Eli lifted her left leg and went as deep as he could. The only sounds to be heard were a melody of grunts, groans, and body fluids being squished between them. Lauren let herself fall into his embrace, giving over all of her resolve and hesitation.

That afternoon, Eli made her climax repeatedly until she pleaded with him to stop. She knew it would be magical once love found her again but never expected it to be packaged in such a way as Eli Sorensen. Just the thought of him made her wet again. The drive back to the resort was a peaceful one, and Lauren glowed from the newfound joy.

Chapter Seven

That night, they opted to stay in. Lauren had no intention of letting anyone or anything spoil the high she was still on. Eli was all too happy to oblige, and they ordered a full spread through room service. They made love in almost every area of the suite. The rest of the time, they strutted around naked, feeding each other.

"Too soon to get a place together when we get back?"

Lauren looked at him with a raised eyebrow.

"Ahhh, well, I already have a place, and I don't plan on shackin' up with any man."

"Who said anything about shaking up? I said get a place together."

"Don't you think this is moving a bit too fast?"

"No. We both know what we want and why prolong

it. If you want to go to marriage counseling, we can, but I've wanted you for a long time, Lauren Shaw. I don't intend to let you go now. My name is Eli, not Marcus."

The sound of Marcus' name made her remember all the times she wasted in a dead relationship. Here, she had the chance to be happy with someone who cherishes her. So, what was the problem?

"How do you think your family will react towards us?"

"If I'm happy and they see you love me, then they'll be overjoyed. Their concerns are the same as mine: finding someone who wants me for me and not what I have."

"I see. I need a little more time to think about this."

"I understand. How about four weeks?"

"Four weeks?"

"That's how long I'll be gone for when we get back home. I need to go to California to wrap up some business deals, and if I'm lucky, maybe I can be back in two. So, do you think that would be enough time to see if this is what you want also?"

"I guess. We'll see."

"Good. Now let me stock up on all your sweetness to tie me over while I'm away," Eli teased gently, pulling at a nipple before taking it in his warm mouth.

By the time they had gotten back to the city the next day, Eli had explored every inch of Lauren's body. True to his word, he resigned on the first day back in the office and worked with Janet on how to run Lauren's affairs. Each night, they did have dinner together, but instead of at her office, they dined at different restaurants around the city.

On the last night before he flew out to California, Lauren cooked dinner for them. It was such a surprise to Eli; he checked the trash for take-out boxes because he had no idea she cooked.

"This is delicious," he said, enjoying the roasted chicken. "I had no idea you knew your way around the kitchen."

"There are still a few things about me you don't know, Eli. Mr. Eli Sorensen," she quickly corrected when he gave her a knowing look. "Are you expecting me to call you that all the time?"

"No, just ever so often when we are making love. I plan to make up for some of the countless times I was required to call you, Ms. Shaw."

Rolling her eyes, Lauren finished her last mouthful of food and went to get the dessert from the fridge. She returned with a large slice of cheesecake and two forks.

"I thought we could share this for dessert?"

"Hmm, looks good and almost as tasty as you."

They took turns feeding cake to each other, never missing the chance to lick crumbs off the other's lips. The night was full of touches, caresses, slow and fast lovemaking, and confessions of deep desires. By the time the sun rose, Lauren was starting to miss him already, though she didn't say it. The next few weeks would tell her if it was all lust or something more.

Eli was heading straight to the airport from her place, and she did her best to act as if it was no big deal that he wouldn't be around like before. Janet had proven to be very efficient, but she wasn't Eli; no one was. The last kiss was etched in her mind as he squeezed her one more time.

"I'll message you when we're about to take off and call you when I arrive. Try not to work late too and eat well. I left Janet instructions to make sure you have as healthy a meal plan as possible until I get back. Think of us, and let me know when you've made your decision." With that, he was gone.

Chapter Eight

Hell, that's what it was without Eli around. Work had leveled out, but the time she was away from the office dragged on. Her once safe hideaway apartment had become a silent tomb without him. In just a matter of days, Eli had flipped her world inside out. *I need a distraction.*

With that, Lauren headed to the gym. On the way there, she sees a realtor having an open house in the building next to it. Since she was looking for anything to take her mind off the stink feelings she was dealing with, she went to check it out. The condo they were showing was a nice three-bedroom split-floor plan. It was fully renovated and had a great view of the city. Walking through, Lauren imagined her and Eli living there but wondered what he wanted in a space. *Ahhh, hold up, are you house hunting now? The man has been gone a whole three days, and you are already mentally married.*

Lauren bolted from the unit and took out her frustrations on the treadmill at the gym. As she exercised, she went over all her concerns, from the age gap, career goals, children, his family acceptance, and hers of the other person. In the end, her sore legs and thirst won over her mind. *We'll revisit this later. Right now, I need food.*

Eli hadn't checked on her since his call when he landed in California. Since then, he gave her space to think. She appreciated it, but at the same time, wondered if it was a sign of him losing interest. Pushing the doubt from her mind, she grabbed some food from the take-out spot on the corner and then headed home. Her phone chimed, indicating she had a new text message. Pictures from Marcus flashed on the screen.

He had sent a few of him and Tiffany on honeymoon, along with a message saying he hopes she finds her happiness also. He went on to say he could tell that Eli deeply cared for her and that she should put aside the pain he caused and give them both a chance to experience the love he now was. The message rang loud in Lauren's mind. Over dinner, she began to give her relationship with

Eli some serious thought. *We need to have a conversation; yeah, there are some things we need to get clear first.*

On the fifth day of being out of town, Eli called her. Lauren was getting ready to leave the office when her cell phone rang.

"Hello, beautiful. How have you been?"

"Hello yourself. I've been good. About to leave the office and head to the gym. How're things going with you?"

"Great, actually. I've secured some deals I was after and may be able to leave sooner than expected. Still, that will depend on what develops next week. Have you been eating healthy?"

"I have. I've even started to cook more."

"Really! Well, I hope to be invited to more home-cooked meals when I get back."

"We'll see."

"Miss me yet?"

"I do. Ahh, I wanted to discuss some things with you, though."

"Sure, ask away."

"What will your family think of us? I mean the age thing and children, do you want any, how soon?"

"My family already knows about us, and children are welcome if they are conceived. I'm fine either way in that area; have no set timetable. How about yourself?"

"I haven't told my family about us, and I feel the same about children. If and when conceived, I will be happy either way."

"So, your family thinks you're still single?"

"My family and I keep our private lives private. Besides, I don't want to get questioned to death until I have the facts."

"And just what facts do you need from me?"

"To know if this is a serious, committed relationship or one where you get to add a notch to your bedpost."

"One, I have no bedposts, and two, seriously, as needing air to breathe."

"I see. Well, what about living arrangements? Do you want an apartment or house?"

"If we're staying in the city, I'd like to get a large place with a city view. If staying more outside the city limits, a house with a nice backyard for enjoying time under the stars. You chose, as I'm good either way."

"I'd like to remain in the city."

"City high-rise condo it is. There are some new ones

about to hit the market in a few weeks, last time I checked. We should go take a look when I get back."

"Okay, sure."

"Wow, didn't expect that to go so smoothly. You must have really been thinking of us."

"I have."

"I miss you, Lauren. I miss us."

"I miss us too."

"Okay, sorry, but I have to go now. My next meeting is about to start, and if I can cut this trip short, I will. Talk to you later."

"Okay, later." Lauren stared at the blank phone screen for a moment, thinking about how easy it was to plan with him. It took her by surprise because all the rehearsing she'd done of how she'd react when he finally called went out the window the moment she heard his voice. *Whipped!*

Eli

He missed her terribly. It had been a challenge to hold out so long before calling her. Sitting in yet another meeting, he forced himself to listen to what was being said. The large hotel bed he slept in felt hard and cold without her next to him. He had it in the worst way for her. Eli made a mental note to send her some flowers before turning his attention to the large flat screen displaying the projected revenues his new business ventures were expected to generate in the coming year.

Once that meeting was over, Eli checked his schedule and moved some things around. If he could reschedule the next two meetings, he could cut his trip short by quite a few days. Anything that came up, he could handle over as many video conferences as needed back home.

"Hi, Dave. Eli here. Wanted to see if we could move up our meeting to either this afternoon, if you're free, or tomorrow?"

"Hey Eli, glad you called. Just so happens that my afternoon opened up. Can you stop by in about an hour or so?"

"On my way, thanks, Dave!"

"Excuse me; I have a delivery for Lauren Shaw."

"Hi, I'll take them, thanks," replied Janet, slightly wide-eyed upon inspecting the 24 long-stem red roses with sprigs of lavender. *That Eli is so romantic. Hmm, these smell so nice. To be in love, ahhh, someday.*

Janet searched Lauren's office for the perfect place to set the heavy vase of fragrant flowers. Settling on the side table near the north-facing window, she stepped back, admiring the view.

"Oh, hi Janet, need something?" Lauren asked, walking into the room while scanning a document.

"No, just finding a home for these beauties."

"What beauties are you….OH, those beauties," Lauren practically giggled, walking closer to inhale the tantalizing aromas.

"Looks like someone is having separation anxiety in California."

"Looks so. I didn't expect another delivery since the usual weekly spring bouquet is already here."

"What can you say? Love will make you do the unexpected."

"Yes, it does. Well, thanks for bringing them in. They look amazing against that window. Would you be so kind as to reschedule my two o'clock for later this week? Thanks."

"Sure, will get right on it."

Lauren sat at her desk, admiring the newly arrived arrangement. Its scent had already started to make its way across the open space. Sweet thoughts of Eli flooded her mind, and hotter ones she tried to keep locked away until he returned. With one more glance at the flowers, she smiled and opened the card that accompanied them. She read the enclosed softly to herself,

"Wine comes in at the mouth

And love comes in at the eye;

That's all we shall know for truth

Before we grow old and die.

I lift the glass to my mouth,

I look at you, and I sigh.

     - A poem by W.B. Yeats."

Lauren smiled and then bit her bottom lip. Her cheeks became flush as she reread the card. Eli certainly knew how to push her buttons, and she'd begun to enjoy falling into his love. *Okay, the mental break is over, Missy.* With that thought, Lauren busied herself with the pile of papers in front of her.

The days seemed to roll into each other, and she did her best to focus on anything but the longing that was just around the corner of every thought. The newly arrived roses and card, though, threatened to shake things up a bit.

It was Friday late morning, and the office was a buzz as everyone tried to meet deadlines so as not to have to come in over the weekend. A soft knock on her office door made Lauren turn from her computer. All she could see was another huge arrangement of red roses and lavender. Beaming, she walked over to help Janet with the load.

"Another one? Now, this is a surprise."

"Where would you like it? Those from two days ago still look as fresh as the day they arrived."

"Umm, let's set them down over here on the credenza."

The two women stepped back near the office entrance to admire the effect the roses had on the space.

"It's starting to look like a garden in here. You deserve it. I'm happy to see you smiling more and working less. Speaking of which, your next meeting should start in about five minutes. I was just informed by the lobby that the clients are on their way up."

"Great, I'll be right there," Lauren said, reaching now for the card sticking out of the arrangement. Softly, she read it,

"If roses were red and violets could be blue,

I'd take us away to a place just for two.

You'd see my true colors and all that I felt.

I'd see that you could love me and nobody else.

- A poem by Kori Frias."

A broad smile took over Lauren's face. Her heart was racing, and the longing she'd managed to keep at bay consumed her. After a series of deep breaths, she reeled in her emotions and mentally prepared for her meeting. *Daydreaming of Eli will have to wait. I need to be at my best today as there's a lot riding on this partnership. Alright, let's do this.* One last mirror check, and she was headed toward the conference room.

By the time Lauren left the office later that day, she'd checked her phone numerous times, but there still were no messages from Eli. Figuring he was still giving her room to think, she decided to send a quick message: *Thank you for the flowers. They're gorgeous!*

Fifteen minutes later, as she exited the building, he replied: *Thanks, glad you liked them. Will be out of service area over the weekend. Check back with you on Monday.*

Looking at the message again, Lauren sighed, preparing herself for another lonely weekend.

Eli

I wonder what type of flowers the florist used this week to get a special thanks for Lauren? Besides, she would have gotten them on Monday, not today. Brushing the thought aside, Eli prepared himself for another meeting with his investors. On the drive to their office, he passed a jewelry store. With a quick U-turn, he went in to see what treasure he could get her.

From memory, he knew she wore only a few pieces. At last count, she had three different pairs of earrings that were alternated throughout the week. Thinking of getting a pair of diamond studs, his eyes were caught instead by a pair of hoops with teardrop-shaped yellow garnets. The color of the stones would complement her skin and hair beautifully. Without hesitation, he purchased them and resumed his journey.

Monday morning came after a weekend of gym and a streamed movie marathon. Lauren had decided to take a much-needed break and do nothing. She opted for all action films as the selection of romances was just too sappy for her to deal with.

Stepping into her office, she was taken aback by yet another arrangement of 24 long-stemmed red roses and lavender sprigs. This time, they were planted on her desk.

Feeling like a child on Christmas morning, she dropped her bag on the nearby chair and reached for the card. She still hadn't heard from Eli yet, but with the three-hour time difference, she guessed he was still asleep.

"Dinner, Chateau De Marquee, 7:30 pm."

Lauren almost squealed with excitement. The thought of seeing Eli made her giddy and a bit afraid at the same time. All the pretend conversations she'd had during his absence were about to be put to the test. Though she knew she cared for him, she still had apprehensions about how others would react. Janet was the only person in the city besides Eli's family who had a clue, and she had sworn to keep quiet.

Mentally going through her closet, she decided on wearing a fitted cream and red dress along with a fairly new pair of nude heels she treated herself to after returning from Marcus' wedding.

"Janet," she called out.

"Yes, Lauren?"

I need to be out of here by 4:00 pm today. If anything is on my calendar after that time, reschedule, please."

"Will do. Sorry, but there was no place else to put the new delivery. The ones from Wednesday are still holding on."

"No worries. It seems I've been summoned to

dinner," Lauren said, beaming with excitement.

"Yes! Finally, he's back. Well, don't worry about your calendar; I'll take care of everything. You go have fun, and if you need to call out tomorrow, just message me," Janet gave Lauren a wink before leaving.

The day dragged as far as Lauren was concerned, despite the tasks she had listed to get done. Lunch was a small bowl of soup, which she had to force down. Her nerves were starting to get the better of her. *Pull it together, girl. Shit, you acting like this is your first date with the man. Though the loving tonight will no doubt surpass all you two have shared to date.*

Lauren arrived at the restaurant 10 minutes early. She sat in her car, trying to keep her mind on the small queue ahead of her in the valet line. Five minutes later, she was walking into the exquisitely French-decorated restaurant.

"Good evening, and welcome to Chateau de Marquee. Your name, please."

"Good evening, Lauren Shaw. I'm meeting my party here at 7:30."

"Yes, Ms. Shaw, right this way, please."

Lauren followed the well-tailored man through the

restaurant. He led her out to the terrace, where there were several patrons lost in conversation, others trying to discretely give her the once over. A chair was pulled out for her at a smaller, intimate setting for two.

"Your party asked if you would kindly wait a moment for their return. May I offer you something to drink?"

"Thank you. Just water, for now, would be fine."

Once her water was served, Lauren was left alone. She glanced over the city view, taking in the skyline and the sounds of the nightlife getting underway. A deep voice pulled her from thought as it danced over her right shoulder.

"Please pardon me. I wanted to put in a special request with the kitchen for my special guest. Thank you for accepting my invitation."

Lauren stopped breathing for a moment at the realization that her date was not Eli; far from it. Doing her best to hide the disappointment and shock, she gave a slight smile and nodded.

"Dante Lloyd of …"

"Standward Sureties, I recognize the name. Thank you for the invitation. I must say it is a surprise. Also, the beautiful roses have made my office resemble a garden this past week, though unnecessary."

"They were the least I could do to get your attention. I'm happy to see they did."

"I'm sorry, Mr. Lloyd."

"Dante, I insist."

"Dante, thank you for the flowers and invitation, but this is quite irregular for me."

"Having dinner is irregular for you," he mused.

"No, that's not what I meant."

"No worries, Lauren. May I call you Lauren?" She nodded a bit reluctantly but had to admit Dante was smooth and undoubtedly used to getting what he wanted. "I desire to get to know you better and figured sending flowers was the least intrusive way of getting you here to dinner."

There was a long pause as each summed the other up. Dante was a handsome Black man, the type Lauren always found herself attracted to. His confidence was sexy as hell, and he was easy on the eyes. The cologne he wore smelt like money, big money, and the flashing white smile he gave her made her body react unexpectedly; she was getting wet.

"Since you're here, looking lovely, I may add, let's at least enjoy the great food and atmosphere. What do you say?"

"Very well," Lauren agreed. She'd gone to a lot of trouble getting ready, and the smell of delicious food was making her remember she barely ate at lunch.

"Good. Would you care for some wine or something else?"

"No thanks; water is just fine. So, tell me, Dante, why the interest in me?"

They spent the rest of the evening discussing a myriad of things. Dante explained he found her to be a puzzle he'd like to solve after looking into her firm during their business negotiations. Much of Lauren's life was not on the Internet. Something she purposely planned. Dante was charming; she had to give that to him, and his knowledge base was vast. It was easy to talk to him and not feel overly threatened by her vault of information.

Without realizing the time had gone by so quickly, Lauren glanced at her watch to see it was approaching 9:30 pm. They had enjoyed a lovely five-course meal and talked about almost everything from finance to tech to politics. She was thankful Dante didn't probe too much about her personal life. *Eli.*

"I enjoyed your company immensely, Lauren. I hope you can say the same about mine?" Dante said softly, this time holding her gaze with eyes that were attempting to drill into her core.

"I did. It was nice to get out and share this wonderful place with someone who can hold a great conversation about things other than strictly finance."

"I can assure you; I'm a man of many surprises and resources. Does this mean we can do this again sometime soon?" Sensing her hesitation, Dante added, "If you are seeing someone else, I would completely understand. My only question is that you consider which one of us meets all the things on your checklist."

"Checklist?"

"Yes, you know, the one every woman carries around inside. I have four sisters, and I know women have a checklist," he replied, shooting her another of his bright, heart-stopping smiles.

"Fair enough. I'll consider your proposal."

"Hmm, proposal. That sounds so formal. I'm trying here to get us on a more personal level."

"I can see that. Well, I must get going. Thank you

again for the lovely evening and gorgeous flowers."

"It is I that should be thanking you. I have been the envy of quite a few men in this place. Would you allow me to escort you outside? It would be the feather in my cap tonight."

With a smile, Lauren agreed, and the two walked out of the restaurant, Lauren taking his arm, looking like a million dollars. She had to admit the evening took her mind off of the loneliness she'd been experiencing with Eli out of town. Dante was great company, but she was well aware of his intent. *No, dinner is all we shall share, Mr. Lloyd. My bed and heart are already occupied.*

Chapter Nine

Lauren arrived home just after 10:00 pm. She took a hot shower and slipped on an oversized t-shirt and a pair of cotton thongs. Her mind had much to sort through, and even though Dante was charming, he proved to be just what she needed. He'd shown here that her heart was full of Eli. Regardless of the age difference and color of their skin, he touched her in the way she desired most. Yeah, she had a checklist but realized no one could complete it; hoping so only made people end up alone.

Checking her phone, she saw there were no messages or missed calls from Eli. *I thought he was going to check in today. Damn, I miss him. When is he coming home?* She dialed his number but got the voice mail.

"Hey, it's me. Just wanted to hear your voice. I miss

you and hope all is going well over there. Kisses."

Eli

Lauren's photo flashed across his cell phone's screen. Eli thought of answering but decided he was in no mood to deal with whatever was going on with her. Janet had slipped about some surprise dinner date and three sets of roses she received. He figured those were the flowers Lauren had texted him about, thinking he'd sent them.

So, while I'm out of town, someone else is making a move on her, and she let them? Why would I send specific flowers like roses when I have a weekly standing order of a spring bouquet already? And dinner; I bet she dressed up for it, too, thinking it was me.

"SHIT," he hissed.

"Mr. Sorensen, Mr. Barker will see you now, right this way."

Eli followed the woman down a hall. He was meeting with his final investor. All things going as hoped, he'd be able to catch a late flight back to the East Coast. If not, he'd be forced to stay in California for another week. *I've got to get back home. I need to deal with these vultures swirling around my woman. Did she sleep with him?*

The meeting was a success, and Eli was taking his seat on the airplane by 7:00 pm that evening. He didn't bother to call Lauren since he still wasn't sure how he'd handle things. Her earlier voicemail still went unanswered, and all he could do was stop letting his imagination run wild thinking of another man holding her, touching and tasting the body that drove him crazy. His heart was pounding at the thought of losing her so quickly. She still didn't give him all the answers he wanted, and the fate of their relationship was unsure.

One step at a time. Just get home, talk to her, and see what's up. No use in letting your thoughts go to unnecessary places. With that, Eli closed his eyes and forced himself to sleep on the long flight. *One way or another, he was keeping her. Too much time and patience went into getting this far with Lauren to give up now.*

The next day, Eli needed to stop by Lauren's office to get some personal forms from the H.R. Department. He still wasn't ready to face her and his emotions yet, so he did his best to avoid being seen by anyone on her team. Almost home-free, he turned the last corner of the hallway before the lobby and almost ran right into her. The look on her face changed from shocked to angry in a flash.

"You're back."

"Yeah, got in late last night. Didn't want to disturb you."

"You know I would have picked up no matter the time."

"Didn't want to intrude on whatever you were doing or who?"

"Who? What are you trying to accuse me of, Eli?" Lauren seethed, looking around to make sure no one could hear them.

"Look, I need to get going; I'm meter-parked."

"Yeah, fine. You do that. Talk to you later?"

"Yeah, later." Eli brushed past her, making a bee-line for the exit.

His evident frustration and coldness had Lauren's mind working overtime. Still unable to figure out what was up with him, she walked past Janet in a daze.

"Hey, you alright, Lauren?"

"Ahh yeah; no."

"What's wrong?" Janet gently questioned, closing the office door behind her.

"I just saw Eli in the hallway. He was trying to leave without seeing me. He was so cold and withdrawn. I don't get it?"

"He kinda knows about the roses and dinner you had last night."

"Kinda?" Lauren replied, starting to shake.

"He called not long after you left the office, and I said how the roses were holding up so well and to have a great time a dinner."

"What?!" Lauren shrieked. "Oh my God, he knows I went on a date with someone else and the flowers. Ooooooooo!"

"I'm sure you can explain it all to him and fix things. He knows men are attracted to you, Lauren."

"You didn't see the way he acted toward me, Janet. It was not the Eli I know, the Eli I thought I knew."

"Men need space and time to handle emotional things. Just give him some; he'll come around."

"Yeah, maybe. Enough of this. Can you take those files from my credenza and have Anthony secure them in the filing room? Thanks."

"Okay, and I'm sorry if what I said caused this misunderstanding. I can call and explain to Eli…"

"No, that's alright, Janet. I'll take care of it."

Eli had been back for more than a week now, and still, Lauren hadn't heard from him, let alone seen him. Since the brief passing in the hallway, her smiling face was slowly being replaced by a scowl, and several of the people at work had taken notice.

Janet did her best to keep things positive, but there was only so much she could do. Lauren needed answers, but Eli was making it clear he wasn't ready to provide any. Dante was a regular phone call at work. He was still working his charm, hoping for more private time with her. Out of frustration, she was tempted to take him up on a lunch offer, but her heart couldn't do it.

She stared at the invitation Janet had left on her desk for a private gallery showing later that evening. It was sent to the company by a client, and since none of the other executives were free, she was stuck with the task of making an appearance.

What the hell? Nothing else is going on tonight. Could be a great distraction. With a new mindset, she headed out the door just after 5:00 pm and rushed home to change. She arrived at 7:00 pm, which was perfect since many of the guests had already shown up.

Just walk around and do a little PR, drink some wine, and bounce. Can you do that without thinking of Eli? Spotting a server, Lauren took a glass of champagne and began her planned course of meandering around the gallery. A lovely oil painting caught her eye. It reminded her of the lookout point she'd gone to with Eli after Marcus' wedding. Lost in her thoughts, she almost jumped when someone gently touched her right elbow.

"Sorry, didn't mean to startle you." It was Dante Lloyd in all his masculine glory. He was wearing a different cologne than before. Still, it made Lauren swoon briefly.

"Well, hello. Didn't expect to see you here."

"I came as a guest of an associate who was personally invited. You?"

"Company invitation fell to me. Here out of

obligation."

They both laughed at her statement, and he joined her as she continued to make her way around the gallery. About twenty minutes later, a large black and white photo hanging on a far wall snatched Lauren's breath away.

The hair, shape of the jaw, and eyes were unmistakable: Eli. He was dressed in nothing more than a pair of worn denim jeans, standing barefoot with his weight shifted on his right leg. Dante was going on about something, and Lauren could no longer hear him. The pounding of her heart filled her ears as she mindlessly walked toward the photo.

"I hear he is a muse for the gallery owner; Eli something or other."

"Sorensen, Eli Sorensen." Just saying his name made Lauren's heartache. She missed him terribly, but he pulled away.

"Yes, that's it. A handsome man, if I must admit. Have you considered spending more time with me yet?" Dante asked hopefully, but Lauren was again lost in thoughts of the times she spent with the specimen staring back at her from the photo.

The sound of someone's voice from behind them

pulled their attention to the other side of the gallery.

"Ladies and gentlemen, thank you all so very much for coming out tonight to share in the opening of my gallery. You honor me with your presence, and please, if you have questions about any piece, don't hesitate to ask my assistants or me. Thank you all again for coming."

"Excuse me, do you know where the restroom is," Lauren turned to Dante and inquired.

"Yes, just around that corner there. I'll be right here when you get back."

Lauren hurried off to the restroom, careful not to bump into anyone. The gallery was still being filled with guests since she arrived. Checking her watch, she had about another twenty-five minutes before her curtesy hour of "show" was up.

Once in the private confines of the toilet stall, she reached into her purse to check her cell phone. No missed calls or messages. *This is ridiculous. Why hasn't he called or tried to get my side of the story? That's it. As soon as I leave this place, I'm heading over to his.*

When Lauren got back out front, she spotted Dante surrounded by several others deep in conversation. Deciding to be free of him, she took a left turn and headed toward a small group surrounding the gallery owner.

A tuft of blond hair turned her head, and a voice she knew all too well pulled her ears to her right. Eli stood talking with two men in front of a metal sculpture. One of them spotted her staring, which prompted Eli to turn around.

His breath caught at the sight of her. She looked so beautiful in the sleeveless light green dress. The color made him think of the earrings he'd gotten for her in California. *Why is she here? Is she alone?* Feeling the weight of the eyes on his back from his friends, Eli took the steps needed to reach her. Gently, he kissed her cheek, something that he noticed she wasn't expecting.

"Hi, how are you?"

"I'm fine. It's you I'm more concerned with. Why haven't you called or stopped by?"

"Got a lot on my mind and been busy."

"I see. Too busy for us; for me?" Eli didn't respond. "Janet told me what she said, and you have to know nothing happened. I thought the flowers were from you, and that's the only reason I accepted the dinner invitation."

"We can discuss this somewhere else at another time."

"When Eli? When you feel like it?"

"I said not here and not now. I will…"

"There you are beautiful. Oh, I see you found Eli. Nice picture of you over there, man. Dante Lloyd," Dante said, offering Eli his hand to shake.

Eli sized him up and shook his hand, watching Lauren's reactions out of the corner of his eye.

"Thanks. It's from a year ago when I was still modeling."

"I see you know Lauren here. Honestly, I think she is the most beautiful thing here tonight, don't you?"

"Yes, she certainly is. How do you know Lauren?"

"Well, Lauren's company and mine have recently partnered together. She handles our portfolio. Honestly, I'm hoping she'll take up my offer to be something more. My showering her with roses at least got me a dinner date."

"Is that so? Flowers are a way to her heart, you say?"

"Could be."

"Well, if you'll both excuse me, I have people I need to get back to. Enjoy your evening." With that, Eli left them, not daring to look at Lauren, afraid his anger and jealousy would get the best of him.

"Nice young man. So, beautiful, how long will you be hanging out here tonight?"

"I'm leaving now, as a matter of fact. I have another engagement."

"I see. Well, how about dinner with me tomorrow night? We can go wherever you want."

"Dante, you are charming, and any woman would be happy to have you as their man. I, however, am not available. I'm sorry, I have to go." Lauren turned and headed for the entrance, not giving Dante any time to respond. She noticed Eli still hadn't looked her way, his back glaring at her as she passed nearby.

Hot tears stung her eyes as she waited for the valet to bring her car around. Once inside, she let them fall, not caring if her makeup got ruined or not. She pulled into traffic and, so consumed with emotion, realized a few minutes later she was headed in the wrong direction. After having to loop around the city, she made it to Eli's apartment almost an hour later.

His car was not in the parking lot, so she waited. Fixing her makeup, she thought of what she'd say now that he had brought her down even lower emotionally than before. Headlights bounced off her rear-view mirror. Eli was home. He didn't seem to notice her car while making his way up to his apartment. Lauren waited a few minutes, then followed him.

After a few seconds of her ringing his doorbell, Eli stood in front of her with a half-unbuttoned dress shirt and slacks. Without a word, he sidestepped and let her in. The door closed, sucking out all the air in the room.

"We need to talk, Eli. Look, I don't know what you think you know, but there is no one else in my life, and had I known the invitation was not from you, I'd never have gone. You left and kept very little contact with me."

"I was giving you space to sort out your feelings, figure out what you wanted."

"I was doing that. When the roses started to arrive, I thought it was you being you. You've always been so sweet and thoughtful, loving and caring."

"Did you fuck him?"

"How dare you?"

"Lauren, DID YOU FUCK him?"

"I will not answer such a question, Eli. How can you think so low of me?"

"I saw the way he looked at you. Hell, he was fucking you right there in the gallery in his mind. Did he take you in his car, his bed, YOUR BED?"

Lauren stared back wide-eyed and seconds away from bursting into tears, but instead, she started to swing her right arm to slap Eli hard across the face. She was too slow; he caught her arm mid-swing.

"How dare you class me with some loose, uncontrollable, no self-respecting woman? Of all the times you've seen men hit on me, how many did I even give a second glance?"

"None, which is why I asked. I know who he is, Lauren, and he has a reputation for being quite charming, plus other things. I also know you were in a vulnerable state when I left, but I'd hoped you could wait for me to get back home."

"I have waited, Eli! I checked my cell phone a million times a day, hoping you'd call, thinking after a while you forgot me."

"I was giving you space. I wanted you to want me, not because I was available and easy access. I wanted you to know within yourself I was the man for you."

"I didn't need all the time you gave me. I knew after only a few days how much I needed you," Lauren said, quietly staring at her feet. "I'm sorry you were made to think I cheated on you, that you meant so little to me."

"You never answered my questions?"

"No, I did not sleep with him," Lauren said, now looking into his eyes as fresh tears rolled out of hers. His face was still plastered in anger and pain.

"That's not what I asked you. I asked if you fucked him?"

"No, no one but you." It was barely audible as the tears and emotions of pain and loss took her.

She pushed past him and let herself out of the apartment. Each of them needed space. Time to sort out how one incident had tested the foundation they were trying to build together. Eli didn't follow her. Instead, he stripped and took a cold shower, thinking of how shit had gotten to this point so fast.

It was 1:00 am, and Eli was still staring at his bedroom ceiling. If he wanted Lauren, he had to make a move now because he could tell she had begun to build back up her wall the moment she pushed past him.

He jumped out of bed and grabbed the gift bag and keys from his dresser. The night air was cool and reminded him of the first time he made love to her. His arousal made the drive feel like forever. When he got to her apartment, he saw her lights were still on inside.

After three rapid knocks on her front door, Eli waited. He wasn't sure how to start things off, but before he could formulate a plan, she was standing in front of him. Hair a mess, eyes swollen, in a short, thin robe tied at the waist. She never looked more beautiful to him. Lauren turned and started to walk back to the sofa. Eli locked the door and took two long strides, pulling her back to him by the waist.

He nuzzled the side of her neck, slowly kissing it while unfastening the belt of her robe. She didn't stop him; she just stood there, allowing him to do whatever he wanted. Without a word, she let the robe pool at her feet. He kissed her back, biting her on each ass cheek while he knelt before her. Slowly, he turned her around.

A trail of soft kisses was left on her legs as he tore off her thong with his hands. She'd begun to tremble from his touch, which only egged him on. *She smells better than I remember,* Eli thought.

He eased two fingers inside her, waiting for her to make a sound. Once she did, he stood, staying bent at the waist long enough to suck at her round breast. They felt like heaven in his mouth. By now, Lauren was slowly grinding his fingers, spreading her legs wider to accommodate him.

Withdrawing his fingers and sucking them clean, he scooped her up and took her to the bedroom. Turning on the light, he laid her on the bed and reached for the jewelry box in the small gift bag he'd brought. She gasped at the sight of the earrings.

Eli was right; the yellow garnets looked great against her skin and hair. Lauren put them on and touched them as Eli undressed. How she missed seeing him naked. Her mouth wanted nothing more than to explore every part of him. But Eli had other plans.

"I'm sorry for ever doubting your faithfulness toward me. I just lost it when I thought all we had started to build meant nothing to you. Can you forgive me for being such a jerk?"

"That depends."

"Depends on what?"

"Whether or not you can get me to say your name."

"Is that all? Well, Ms. Lauren Shaw, prepare your voice to be shouting my name until sunrise."

True to his word, Eli had Lauren shouting his name. He tortured her with his fingers, tongue, and an erection that wouldn't go down. They tried as many positions as their bodies would allow. With each climax, Lauren fell deeper into his love, and Eli was only too happy to catch her fall.

Within three months, they were moved into a lovely new high-rise apartment with a wall of windows overlooking the city they both loved. Eli had continued to shower Lauren with adoration and affection. He proposed the day they closed on the unit. Lauren had learned to trust the process and not hound him about marriage. She knew Eli was a man of his word, and when he popped the question at lunch in the apartment's rooftop bistro, she blurted out,

"Yes, Mr. Eli Sorensen," before the waterworks took control.

When Eli stood, he held her in his arms and kissed her for a long time. That kiss promised her a lifetime of more love to come, and when he broke free, his blue eyes sparkling in the daylight, he whispered,

"I see you've learned how to say my name well, Ms. Lauren Shaw. Now I have to work on retraining you to say, Daddy."

Everyone around who saw the proposal clapped and cheered. Lauren finally stopped crying and began to smile, thinking of how life had given her, at last, the love of her dreams. *I look forward to being trained, Daddy,* she thought as they made their way out of the bistro.

♥ Thank you for your support. ♥

**Please take a moment and leave a review.
It'd be much appreciated.**

About the Author

A romance lover, Tizahmi works to tell stories of people taking wonderful, sometimes unexpected journeys to find 'the one.' It could be a straight shot or a rollercoaster ride. With love, you never know. Each tale, dripping with Level 3 or 4 Heat.

Writer of contemporary, paranormal, and alien romance stories, Tizahmi welcomes and values all feedback and is honored by your support. Please leave reviews of Tizahmi's books and connect with her via her website and social media accounts. Keep up to date with Tizahmi's latest offerings and events by connecting on social media at: @Tizahmi_Author

Read More from Tizahmi

www.ingramcontent.com/pod-product-compliance
Lightning Source LLC
Chambersburg PA
CBHW050955050726
47592CB00007B/2587